Animals and Friends
Book one

KIMBA THE
KITTEN

PAMELA GRIFFITHS

First published 2022

ISBN:9798750755523

Classification: Short story

Website: www.pamelagriffiths.com

Forward

Following the success of my ten Bossy The Bunny children's books, I've decided to carry on writing for young children. I am pleased to say that I have started a new series of books 'Animals and Friends'.. Book one is entitled Kimba The Kitten.

Pamela Griffiths

DEDICATION

For my partner Sandy Hoffman
And all my family and friends

For all the people who have read my books and
encouraged me to carry on with my writing

Thank you

Pamela Griffiths

ACKNOWLEDGMENTS

I would like to thank all my family and friends for
supporting me throughout my writing years.
It is much appreciated.

I would also like to thank my readers who have continued
to support me by purchasing my books and giving me
reviews and feedback I thank you all.

Pamela Griffiths

Animals and Friends
Book one

Kimba the kitten

Kimba The Kitten

Kimba is a kitten cat
A baby furry ball

She sits upon the window sill
So she can see it all

She watches very closely
as people pass her by

Kimba is inquisitive
she's always asking why

Her owners have adopted her
They brought her to their home

Kimba felt quite frightened
Until lots of love was shown

Now Kimba loves to be there
She can play and bounce around

Kimba rolls across the floor
With a piece of string she found

Her owners take good care of her
She has a nice soft bed

Kimber likes to sleep in it
Or on the settee instead

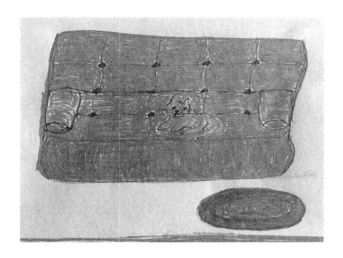

Kimba is a happy cat
She is always having fun

From waking up she plays
Until the day is done

Her owners have two children
Who love to play with her

They get her lots of kitten toys
And they stroke her fluffy fur

Kimba eats her cat food
From her own special bowl

She gets her food when hungry
All she has to do is call

She can't talk like the humans
But she can make them understand

When she is hungry or thirsty
Humans make her feel so grand

Kimba is a precious cat
She rules her owners house

Loving all the attention
As she chases a little mouse

She is settling in quite nicely
There is so much to see and do

Her owners got her a litter tray
'Here's a toilet just for you'

Kimba's toilet is private
A box with a flapping door

It was placed in a corner
In the porch down on the floor

In the litter tray there is gravel
Kimba scats it around its good

Now when she needs a toilet
Kimba uses it like she should

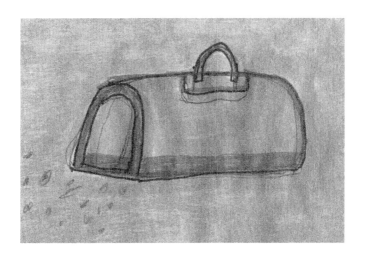

Life is so exciting now
Kimba likes to explore new things

Her owners are very kind people
Who knows what tomorrow will bring

Kimba sits by the window
Waiting for treats today

The children will be home soon
And then they all will play

Kimba spots a little bird
She makes funny noises at this

Its not a normal meow sound
It sounds more like a hiss

When the humans left for work
Kimba saw a shelf up high

It had lots of lovely ornaments
If only she could fly

One day she would climb up there
She wasn't big enough yet

But that is for the future
Those ornaments she would get

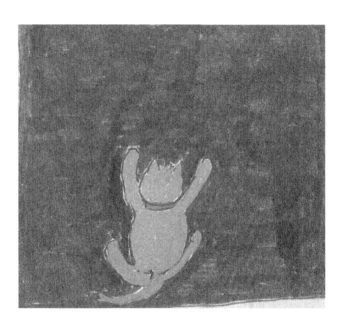

Everything was new to her
Kimba had the time of her life

Jumping and rolling everywhere
Causing a lot of strife

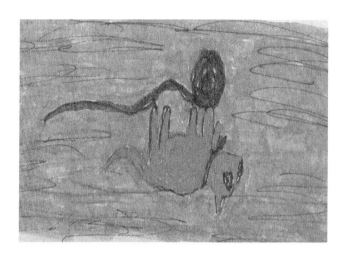

Kimba sat and washed her fur
She is a very clean cat

Looking good makes her happy
So there's nothing wrong with that

Every day is a surprise
Something new comes her way

Kimba lays in her comfy bed
Waiting for what comes today

Her owners bring her lovely toys
Kimba loves to run and play

A clockwork mouse she chases
She tries to scare it away

A spider crawls along the floor
Kimba wants it to stay

The spider doesn't want to
So it quickly runs away

Kimba likes her fur to shine
Her owners brush her fur

Every day she loves this
It means so much to her

When it rains outside
Kimba likes to stay inside

She doesn't like getting wet
So she finds a place to hide

Kimba the kitten is happy
She loves her forever home

Living with her new family
She will never feel alone

When the children return from school
She purrs and rubs through their legs

Meowing to get their attention
Please play with me she begs

Kimba loves her new home
She is very happy there

Her home is filled with love
Where her owners give her care

Kimba is a lucky kitten to have found such a loving
family. Always love and be kind to animals and they
will always love you too.

ABOUT THE AUTHOR

Pamela Griffiths nee Cocker was born in Sheffield in September 1952; Widow of Clive Griffiths. She has three children, a stepson, nine grandchildren and 3 great granddaughters and 2 great grandsons. Pamela has a diploma in freelance journalism, a diploma in quality management and is retired from working for the NHS as a Quality and Development Manager. She lives in Loxley, Sheffield with her partner Sandy Hoffman.

Pamela won a National Local Poetry competition in 2011 with 'Home Sweet Home in Loxley Valley'. She has also won the National Poetry competition 'Great Britain' with her poem 'The Best of British' in 2016. Her winning poems were chosen from many thousands of entries. Her work has been published in over seventy poetry anthologies. Pamela's own poetry books include 'Expressions of Life', 'Moments in Time', 'Life is a Spiral Staircase', A Sheffield Lass', 'Under a Blood Red Moon' and 'Fur Babies'.

Over the years Pamela has donated and contributed many of her books for various charities and fund raising events.

For more information please visit:

Website - www.pamelagriffiths.com
Twitter - @pamg56
Author fan page on Facebook - Author Pamela Griffiths

Printed in Great Britain
by Amazon

81574809R00031